# THE SOCIETY OF ANGELS:

## A Nephilim Conspiracy

By

**Rodolfo Molina**

# Dedication

*"To my wife and life partner, Dr. Blanca C. Molina."*

# Contents

*Page Is Left Blank Intentionally*

# Chapter 1

The desert heat was not something Dr. Gallo was accustomed to. He wiped the sweat off his brow. His head hurt, and his lips were chapped. He was thirsty and even more tired. He wanted, at that moment, nothing more than a good restful sleep. The cave wasn't as hot as it was on the outside, but it was humid, and he was having his good share of trouble breathing.

His head hurt as if he had been fighting beasts. His lungs gasped as if he had been smoking for an eternity. Maybe he was tired; he hadn't had a good rest in a while. He had been traveling a lot, meeting people, and, before that, doing extensive research. He needed a break, but at this discovery, he knew he couldn't afford one.

He walked some until he climbed out of the cave, and the gloriously sleeping sun kissed his face. His eyes and forehead, however, were shadowed by the sand-filled, now-beige hat he wore. The sun was setting as it spread its remaining rays of light across the dunes of Jordan. His shadow stretched across, back into the cave. The air was now colder than it was when he entered the cave. It gave him peace and a remedy for his tired body.

He took a step, but his body stumbled as blood rushed to his head, and so he took a moment to regain consciousness. Meanwhile, he looked around and navigated where he was meant to go henceforth.

The never-ending dunes of Jordon witnessed something; the unyielding eyes of Dr. Gallo were where they needed to be: the goat herders east of where he stood. He took a deep breath and reminded himself that east, at the farmhouse, was where he parked his car earlier the dreadful day. It was also the place where it started: the farmhouse, and the boy who found this cave… and the scroll.

***

## Weeks Earlier

Dr. John Gallo paced in no particular hurry, but the chilling air froze him, and right now, nothing concerned him more than finding his way inside the warm halls of Georgetown University. It was Thanksgiving week; everyone seemed to be in a hurry, pacing in and out of the halls of the college. Dr. John Gallo found his way, finally, inside the halls of Georgetown and, as usual, was mesmerized by the gothic architecture of the place. The towering spires, the detailed stonework, the history. There, he walked some more to be where he intended: the Department of Theology and Religious Studies, a place quieter than the library. Dr. John Gallo is a Jesuit and the youngest professor but is known for his knowledge in Theology. In his rather short tenure, he had achieved three PhDs in Theology from Harvard, Archeology from Oxford, and Historical Linguistics from Stanford.

A broad smile on his face, a perfume that smelled too nice in the air, and Thanksgiving to look forward to were all he needed to get going. He passed by Dr. Jack Murphy, who was the oldest professor in the department. Dr. Murphy was respected and very well-known for his work comparing the present-day Bishop's role to the Apostles of Jesus. The work alone, with extensive research, took him 15 years to complete. It was his model that was now studied all across the world. But for his age, people worried a lot about him. He worked the most, and his old age was not having any mercy on him.

"Good morning, Professor Murphy," Dr. Gallo greeted him with a lively tone. To his surprise, Dr. Murphy, in his office, was dissolved into his studies, reading yet another scripture text with a wooden magnifying glass. When no response came, Dr. Gallo loudly said, "Greetings, Brother Jack."

Dr. Murphy was startled, but soon, his eyes widened from joy upon seeing the young, familiar face of his co-worker. "Did I have you standing there again?"

"Not for long," he replied, patiently with his smile still there. "I was saying my Good morning to you."

"Any morning I wake up to is a good one. It's a joy to be alive, my brother." He began cleaning his glasses with a pocket-sized microfiber cloth. He wore his glasses and laughed, "You're as young as you were yesterday."

"So are you, Dr. Murphy." With a smile, he continued his journey down the halls, greeting and nodding at anyone who crossed his path.

"Cowboys and Commanders this Thursday, Go Commanders!" He said out loud, his hands in the air.

"Ahh, if only they could command a win?" Marge, the Department's invaluable secretary, teased him.

"You never know what tomorrow has in store for us, Miss Marge," he winked at her. 'You look lovely as usual.'

"Careful now, Dr. Gallo. My husband might not find it funny," she fiddled with the pile of papers, a smile still on her face.

Finally, after a short walk to his office and a few more Good Mornings, he was in his small office. There, two familiar faces, his graduate students, Aaron Blaine and Beth O'Connor, awaited him. Aaron was a tall and blonde man with a bright future ahead. He was recently accepted to Harvard Law and studied ethics and philosophy. Aaron was singular-minded; from the day he met Dr. Gallo, he told him of his dream of being a Supreme Court justice, and to this day, not once did he waver. This was something he learned from his professor as he, too, was adamant about doing what he wanted, and so far, he has succeeded. Beth, a five-foot-four-inch brunette with an athletic figure, on the other hand, was the opposite; she believed the world was complicated and not as binary as Aaron thought it to be. She was convinced that no answer was wrong and truth is what one believes in, hence the many religions in the world.

Like her professor, she was studying Theology and is currently working on her Ph.D. thesis: 'The Origin of Ethics and the Role of Major World Religions.' Her work was beyond just earning a name for herself but she hoped, sincerely, to make some inroads into the role of women in the Roman Catholic Church.

"The Roman Catholic Church is in desperate need of a woman's touch," she lectured Aaron while he remained fixated on the Rubik's cube he carries everywhere. 'I am against the excommunication of the Danube Seven, but..."

She snatched the cube from Aaron who was laid back, "Are you even listening, Aaron?"

"Yes!" He replied in annoyance, trying to reach for his Rubik from Beth. "Excommunicated. Very sad. Now, give me back my cube."

Aaron loved to multi-task, and given that Beth was a talker he could not be doing nothing but only listening to her never-ending lectures. He mostly enjoyed video games, but given that he could not carry them everywhere, he made a habit or particularly an obsession with the cube to help him keep his sanity. Still, he is always ears when Beth is talking because he knows Beth hates when he is not listening.

After much struggle, he gives up and sighs. "I wish I was jogging right now. I can't believe I skipped it to be here with you..."

"Talking about excommunications so early in the week?" Dr. Gallo unloaded his briefcase on the lab table. The two who were fighting for the Rubik sat composed now at Dr. Gallo's sofa.

"Well, I was practicing so I could debate better with you," Beth answered.

"Beth, I have a better debate for you: the trip to *Paris*," the professor gleamed at the thought. "This conference on Theology and Law should present us with plenty of information on the topics of religion, the role of women, and how laws are changing this landscape. And all of this, coming from some of the leading scholars in the world."

Listening to Dr. Gallo talk the two couldn't contain their excitement, the cube no longer interested them.

"Eat as much turkey as you desire this Thanksgiving, but leave plenty of room for some fabulous French cuisine. I know some great places to go to in Paris, and I look forward to treating both of you in the city that was once referred to as a movable feast."

"Ahh, I can hardly wait," said Aaron. "I always dreamt of jogging the streets of France. So, refreshing."

"French streets are known for romantic walks, not running!" Beth scolded Aaron. "I can't wait, Dr. Gallo. Feeding mind and body, it can't get any better than that."

"So, what's the plan for this short week, Dr. Gallo?" asked Aaron.

"Just get your papers ready to travel. Organize your notes, and I will forward you the syllabus for next week's conference."

The two nodded. "I still have some work to do on my presentation at the conference. That means the two of you are to meet me at the airport on Sunday afternoon. You both have my cell to call or text me beforehand if needed?"

The two nodded again and did not utter a word. "Good, this means you two are to leave me to my work."

The excitement left their body when asked to leave, as nothing is more fun for them than debating with him. But joy and excitement soon returned with the anticipation of going to Paris. The two departed with a promise to meet at the airport with all the necessary documents.

# Chapter 2



**Monday, A Week Later**

The overnight flight to Paris was uneventful, and despite feeling a little jet-lagged, they all were excited to be there. Standing outside the airport, Aaron, with a slumped stature, waved at a cab. "What are you doing?" Asked Dr. Gallo in a strangely energetic tone. Aaron and Beth looked at him cluelessly as if it wasn't obvious enough that they were waving for a cab. "It's a 5-minute walk to the taxi stand, let's just walk to there and a get a taxi then, it will be within the budget," said professor. "If I walk for even a minute, I will collapse," Beth groaned tiredly. "Same," Aaron chimed in.

Dr. Gallo scoffed, mocking them with his grin. "C'mon, it's near..." Aaron and Beth tiredly walked along the professor. As soon as they arrived at the stand, they hurriedly stuffed into the taxi. Though the taxi driver was a little chatty, they were tired and didn't respond to him back with the same energy, except the professor. During the taxi ride, both Aaron and Beth slept, but the professor was talking to the driver, talking about the new developments in the area. As soon as they arrived at the hotel, they hurriedly dropped off all their luggage and had a quick change of attire for the meeting then took another taxi to the conference site. This ride was a short distance from the hotel that they would have ordinarily walked had they not been so jet-lagged. The conference was scheduled to start at 10:00 am at the Sorbonne, also known as the University of Paris.

At 10:15, they embraced their presence at the University of Paris. Dr. Gallo wore his favorite, well-tailored navy-blue suit and a jacket fitting him just right without being too tight or loose. Beneath, he wore a light blue dress shirt to his otherwise formal appearance and a simple, dark gray tie. Beside him, Aaron wore a charcoal gray blazer over a crisp white shirt, leaving the top button open. Beth chose a classic knee-length black dress, and a light gray cardigan was draped over her shoulders with a small silver pendant hung around her neck.

"Seems like we are the early ones," Beth commented, looking at Dr. Gallo.

"Yes," Aaron jumped in. "I could have slept an hour more."

"Slow down with the complaints. These are the people you will have today. The attendance is kept short for the first day. This is so we can acquaint ourselves with important people and catch up with old friends. Tell you the truth, the fewer the people, the more you enjoy."

"You seem very friendly at work. I always took you for being sociable and that you find it easy to talk to people," Beth said.

"I feel very comfortable speaking to this group. Many of them are good friends and mentors, as well as former collaborators. Some are politicians, and others have a strong background in art. All of which you will find interesting and I would encourage you both to interact with as many as possible.

Beth and Aaron quietly listened as Dr. Gallo was an overly energetic and highly confident person, or so they thought he was. Hearing him share his thoughts on *people* was rare to non-existent.

"Anyway," he took a deep breath. "Let's move."

"Whose lecture are we attending?" Aaron asked as they followed behind fast-stepped Dr. Gallo.

"None in particular," replied Dr. Gallo. "Today is all about awards and recognition. This will be good for you two; you will get to know the brief history of these people and, more importantly, know with whom you are to connect."

As they headed to the auditorium, Dr. Gallo felt a light tap on his shoulder. "I assume your flight was a pleasant one, dear friend."

Surprised, Dr. Gallo returned his smile. "Of course, it was, Professor James Hearst! It's been a while; I was searching your face among the crowd."

"If you were, you would have found me already. I am too tall to be hidden." The two shared a peal of laughter. "I just got here a minute ago. How is your research on the Dead Sea Scrolls, any new evidence or the mention of the New Testament?" He leaned his ear at Dr. Gallo for answers.

"I ask you for your patience, my hasty friend," he chuckled. "I know you want to get a preview of my work, but it'll have to wait till Friday. I will tell you this… its new, never been heard before. You are in for a new world."

The reply left a smile of wonder and amusement on his face. "Nothing less to be expected of you. See you around then."

By 4 pm, they left the university and decided to have an early dinner at a nearby café. Dr. Gallo convinced them that it was the cheapest among the rest and that it overlooks the river, and during the night, the glimmers of lights followed by a cold breeze make wine the best drink in the world. They made plans for the morning and decided to have breakfast at the hotel.

"Important lectures start at 10. So, the same schedule as today sounds good?" Dr. Gallo suggested as they entered the elevator in the hotel lobby, to which both of them nodded.

"Dr. Gallo…" a voice called his name in urgency. "You have a message from your office at the front desk," Dr. Gallo stepped out of the elevator, leaving Aron and Beth to continue as decided.

The message was from his friend Professor Amer Hassan. They met at Oxford while both were pursuing their post-doctorate degree in archeology. Professor Hassan was now teaching in the Department of Archeology at the University of Jordan in Amman. Both maintained a close relationship and had been guests at each other's universities, discussing and presenting their research to the faculty members.

They both shared a common interest in their studies of the Dead Sea Scrolls. Professor Hassan left a callback number and a note that read, *"Must talk to you ASAP; I have come into possession of something very important."* The note had a sense of both urgency and excitement, and Professor Hassan was not one to get so easily excited, thought Dr. Gallo.

It was late, and the phone number in the message was of the Department of Archeology at the University of Jordan. When he called, there was no answer, so he thought it would be best to call again in the morning.

He unpacked, took a shower, and then laid down in his bed. He could feel the energy and tension in his muscles fade away. And with that, he faded into a deep and restful sleep.

# Chapter 3



The next day, Dr. John Gallo woke up at 6:00 a.m. with a sense of refreshing energy all over him. If he were in Georgetown, he would be continuing his usual routine of an early morning jog. A habit he had adopted during his time in Georgetown. But a recent message from a dear friend shifted his focus, and he decided to give him a call again. It was the number of the Department of Archeology at the University of Jordan.

When the Department of Archaeology's secretary answered the phone, she interrupted his introduction with a brisk, "Yes, the Professor is expecting your call. Let me transfer you to his office." The line clicked.

Sitting at his desk, he answered, "Yes, who is this?" Finally, a familiar voice came through.

"It's John, Amer. What is this message about my friend?"

"John, it's so good to hear your voice," said Professor Amer Hassan, his tone brimming with excitement. "I have some exciting news for you. Last week, a goat herder's son was tending to his goats. It had rained heavily the night before, and the ground was soft. The boy followed one of the goats to a nearby rock outcrop near the desert. As the boy stood up on the rock, he slipped to the ground. But the ground under him collapsed into a cave. There, in the cave, the boy found an unmarked vase. He was unhurt and was able to climb out of the cave and go to get his father. The boy and his father are good friends of mine, so they removed the vase from the cave and brought it to me. Fortunately, their farm is not far from here. John, the vase, it's in excellent condition, and it has, I believe, the complete Book of

Enoch, written in ancient Hebrew or should I call it Biblical Hebrew."

John's curiosity was piqued, and they continued, "This must be Cave number 13, and just like the Bedouin boy's discovery of Cave number one, so was this one found." His voice was getting serious, "But this is very strange. The only version of the Book of Enoch in existence today was written in an ancient Ethiopian dialect, as you know, my friend, and that version has some gaps. This scroll is written in ancient Hebrew, but there is something even more strange about this finding."

"What do you mean?" Dr. Gallo replied.

Amer's tone grew more serious. "With the scrolls, in the vase, a metal object shaped like a dagger with a handle was found. I say dagger, but there is no sharp end. It is blunted at the tip, and it has no sharp edges; it's more rounded, and the bolster is round with a circular indentation, and it has no markings. I just don't understand its purpose."

Dr. Gallo, though intrigued, was somewhat puzzled. "Well, that's a first," sounding perplexed. "' I'm not sure I understand its meaning or why it's even there, but perhaps this will be explained in the scroll?"

Amer, with urgency in his voice, insisted, "John, you must come. I cannot think of anyone else who knows more about the Book of Enoch than you."

John's excitement bubbled over. "What are you saying? Are you telling me what I think you are saying?"

With the same energy, the professor replied, "Yes, I think we are saying the same thing. That is why I called you and no one else."

"Amer, I would love to be the one to translate this scroll. It's an honor, my friend." Gallo replied with humility.

Pausing, Gallo asked with impatience, "So, you think I would be able to bring the scroll to my lab in Georgetown to complete the translation?"

"I understand," said Amer. "I'll make all the necessary arrangements. Just come as soon as you can."

John, feeling the excitement of the prospect of translating a complete version of the Book of Enoch, thought to himself, this is a scholar's dream.

"Let me check for flights from Paris to Amman today. I won't be able to stay long. I have two graduate students with me, and I am giving a talk at the plenary session this Friday. This brings me to an obvious question: Why aren't you here?" Asked Dr. Gallo.

Apologetically responding, Amer said, "I was planning to go, but when this finding was presented to me, I could not think of anything else."

"I understand my friend. I'll let you know about my flight and my arrival after I make all the arrangements," replied John.

Amer, with excitement, "I will pick you up, and I must show you something before coming to my office to inspect the scrolls."

"What?" John asked out of curiosity.

"You'll see." Replied the professor in a mysterious tone.

After such an intriguing conversation, there was a mix of emotions inside him. He was curious and excited, but importantly, he was humbled that this opportunity could have been given to anybody, but it came to him. He was thankful. He went to the hotel breakfast room, waved to the waitress, and, in French, ordered a coffee at his table, where he saw Aaron and Beth sitting, already eating, and arguing about the morality exhibited by great apes.

Aaron waved his hands as he continued his argument with Beth, "Just look at how the great apes understand parity. That is not taught; it's innate."

He was about to continue when he was interrupted by Beth, "Parity, that's behavior, not morality." As always, she came back with a more vital viewpoint.

When Dr. Gallo joined them, the conversation paused. Both Aaron and Beth looked up expectantly.

Aaron, taking a bite of his toast, said, "The buffet is great. Dr. Gallo." Beth said, "And the café au lait, wonderful."

Just then, the waitress delivered Dr. Gallo's coffee. He took a sip, relishing the rich flavor, and said, "I have some great news and not-so-great news for both of you." Aaron and Beth paused and sat silent, waiting for the news.

Taking another sip of his coffee and removing a toast from Aaron's plate, he took a bite of it, saying, "Yum, this is good. Brioche? Well, the great news is that I just got off the phone with my friend Professor Amer Hassan, from the University of Jordan. He has in his possession a recently found Dead Sea Scroll, the Book of Enoch, and he tells me it's complete and in pristine condition. He wants me to go to Jordan, pick it up, and bring it back to Georgetown for its complete translation."

He then sat back in his chair, smiling and with a look of contentment and expecting high fives from his students, but instead, he saw them contemplating the news.

Aaron, intrigued, asked, "What's the not-so-great news?"

Dr. Gallo sighed. "I have a flight leaving in an hour, and I'll be gone for the rest of today and most of tomorrow. You'll be on your own in Paris."

Aaron grinned. "Two days in Paris without a 'chaperone'? Sounds like an adventure. Moulin Rouge, here we come!" Beth, less enthusiastic about the idea of a whirlwind tour, said, "Mona Lisa, the Louvre, Musee d'Orsay and a walk-up Montmartre, that's what I would like to do."

Dr. Gallo, a bit taken aback by their differing reactions, said, "Let's not forget the conference. Alright, I get it. It's Paris. Nonetheless, my friend Dr. James Hearst from Oxford is here and you can call him if you get yourselves into any trouble. Here's his number. Okay, I have to go. I have a taxi waiting for me and tomorrow when I return, let's have dinner. We will regroup then." He got up, took another sip of his coffee, and kept the rest of the toast in his hand. He waved goodbye to his students, who were enjoying the moment.

As he stepped into the waiting taxi, he couldn't help but think about the monumental task ahead and the rare opportunity it represented. He hoped his students would make the most of their time in Paris, and he looked forward to reuniting with them and sharing his discoveries upon his return.

# Chapter 4

Although the flight to Amman from Paris is just about five and a half hours, to Gallo, it was like a never-ending ride. All the flight, he was just thinking about this new discovery and all the results that could come out of it. Though he tried to distract himself with a wonderful view of clouds, again, his mind started to boggle over the book of Enoch and what could be found in it. When he arrived at the terminal, his friend Amer was waiting for him desperately.

Amer, in his early 40s, had a medium build, a dark beard, and a receding hairline, but his joyful eyes and inviting smile made him instantly approachable. "Welcome, my friend!" he called out to Gallo. "Come, I have the car parked just outside. We are going to my friend's goat farm, where the cave was found. We won't be able to go tomorrow. My friend has to take his wife to a doctor's appointment, and it would be rude for us to go on his land in their absence. I wanted you to see it for yourself, the cave, and they are expecting us." He continued talking on their way to the car.

They arrived at the farmhouse, where Amer's friend Omar greeted them warmly. His son, Ali, came running from inside the house to see who the newly arrived guests were. They spoke in Arabic, and the boy pointed to a small hill west of their farmhouse and smiled brightly, "Like to see the cave?" He asked in broken English. His father, with a broad smile on his face, proud of his son's ability to speak in English, looks at Professor Hassan and says in Arabic to follow him.

"The cave is not far from here, and we can walk to it," Amer said to John as they set off. When they came upon the cave, Dr. Gallo asked Omar if it would be okay if he entered. Omar nodded yes and gestured with his arms and both hands, pointing to the opening of the cave, granting his request. Amer and John stepped inside one after the other, quickly realizing the cave was much larger than they had expected. When they reached the floor, they realized the cave was larger than they expected. Amer, already familiar with the cave, brought with him two powerful flashlights to explore the floor and the walls of the cave.

Inside the cave, the temperature was a little cooler than the ambient temperature outdoors, and it smelled damp and musty. As they examined the cave floor, they noticed an indentation near the wall where a vase had rested for over a thousand years. There were no other indentations on the floor so both surmised there had been only one vase in this cave. Amer had brought his camera and was busy taking pictures of the cave and the area where the vase once laid.

After thanking Omar and Ali, who stood proudly by the cave's entrance, they returned to the car and headed to Amer's office, where the ancient scrolls were safely stored. Upon arriving, they found most of the staff had gone home for the day. Amer led John to his office, which was filled with books stacked everywhere. There were different artifacts and maps at various locations. There was an empty table in his large office that seemed to have no function. Despite the apparent clutter, John sensed a purposeful order in the chaos set by Amer.

A small safe behind Amer's chair caught John's attention. Amer swiveled his chair around, dialed the combination, and opened the safe. He reached for cotton gloves located on top of the safe, and with his gloved hands, he retrieved the scrolls. He walked the scrolls to the empty table to lay them down and asked John to put some gloves on.

Staring in almost disbelief and excitement, John was astonished by how remarkably well-preserved the scrolls were. Each delicate fold and complicated script seemed to tell a bigger story, untouched by the passage of time. As he began examining the ancient text with a magnifying glass, he was thrilled with anticipation coursing through him. He looked up at Amer, his eyes wide with wonder, and exclaimed, "Remarkable preservation. This is much more complete and it looks like it has an added section that is not present in the Ethiopian version. I would have to confirm that, of course." His heart raced at the thought of discovering new insights from these ancient words, feeling as though he was standing on the brink of a significant discovery.

Amer, stroking his beard and feeling confident about getting his friend John involved, said, "This makes it an important find." Then, with some exclamation, "Very important!". Looking at John, "Oh John, I knew you were the right man for this job."

Looking away from the scrolls and pointing the magnifying glass at Amer, John asked, "What about the metal object that was found in the vase?"

Looking at John and pointing his finger to the safe, "Yes, yes, let me get it."

When he brought the metal object to John, both stared at it with a look of wonder. Lifting it from Amer's grasp, he gave Amer a surprised look, "It's very light. Not at all what I expected, and yes it looks like a dagger with a handle but with a blunt tip. Certainly not a cutting tool or a true dagger." He scrutinized the cross-guard, noting its unusual design. The craftsmanship was evident, suggesting it was made with purpose. He continued, "The cross-guard is also shaped differently. It has a cup-like features facing the tip." "What is this thing?" He wondered aloud.

Scratching his head, Amer gazed at the metal object, a frown creasing his brow. "You know, my friend Nasser studied metallurgy; he's quite the expert on the composition of metals. But these days, there's little money to be made in that field, so he ended up working for the

Department of Tourism. It's a miserable job, but it pays the bills." He paused, recalling the events that led to their current situation.

"So, as I was saying, I loaned this blade, or whatever you want to call it, to him… to study it. He took it home, where he still had some tools to study metals. He bought it back the next day, complaining that this object had destroyed three of his best diamond blades while he was trying to get some shavings for further analysis."

Amer's expression darkened as he continued, "When he asked how I came into possession of it, I told him the whole story. He grew increasingly concerned and now wants nothing to do with it. I never knew he was such a superstitious man."

Puzzled by the metal object's hardness and lightweight, John asked, "May I also take it with me to Georgetown? Perhaps I can find someone there who could help identify its makeup?"

"Yes, yes, of course, it's part of the package," Amer replied.

John, still holding the metal object and examining it, smiled and, nodded his head and said, "Perhaps the complete Book of Enoch will reveal its purpose or meaning. What happened to the vase?"

Pointing to his office's open door, he said, "It's behind the door. It has no markings, just a simple vase."

John moved the door and saw a simple vase that had no pretension of being important or that its contents had anything of value.

He moved the door back to the open position, hiding the vase behind it, and just muttered, "Hmm."

John and Amer gathered all the materials necessary to protect the scroll and put them in a small carry-on luggage. They then went to Amer's home, where his wife had cooked John's favorite dish when visiting Jordan, *mansaf.* "No one makes *mansaf* better than my wife." Boasted Amer.

During dinner, Amer received a phone call, "Who could that be? Calling at this late hour," exclaimed Dana.

Amer stood up, "Don't worry, I'll get it," said Amer. When he returned to the dinner table, his mood had changed to a more serious tone, but he continued to enjoy their recollections from their time at Oxford.

"Amer, the phone call, anything important," asked Dana.

"No, nothing important," Amer said, a smile spreading across his face as he deftly shifted the conversation to Dana's culinary talents. Gallo took another bite from his plate, savoring the flavors. "This is absolutely wonderful, as usual. You truly are the best cook I know, Dana. When will you finally open your own restaurant?"

Dana smiled with pride, "Thank you, John! But honestly, what I enjoy most is hearing you and Amer recount the same stories every time you visit. That brings me more joy than you know."

After dinner, John called for a taxi to take him back to his hotel. Just as he was about to step into the cab, Amer came out from his house, he seemed serious. "John, wait a moment," he called out, stepping forward to speak with him.

Looking worried, Amer continued, "I didn't want to tell you this in front of Dana because you know she worries about everything, but it was my friend, Omar, the goat herder you met, who called me during dinner. He told me he had two men in black suits come to his house soon after we left. They asked about the vase. He told them he knew nothing about its contents and that he delivered it to the University where it belonged. They left without asking anything else, and they did not identify themselves. He wanted to warn me, and now I'm warning you."

"Do you have any idea who these men could be or what they want?" John asked in a concerned tone.

"No, this is the first time I hear of such a thing. But I will let you know if I hear anything more." "Okay, my friend. Good night." Said Amer in a heavy tone while tapping John's back.

Gallo returned to his hotel. He had a restless night.

# Chapter 5

His flight departure time was in the late morning, and he would make it just in time to have dinner with his two students. He was excited to share the news of the scrolls. When he arrived at the airport, he made a phone call to his hotel leaving a message for his students to meet him in the lobby of the hotel at 6:00 pm for dinner. His treat.

At 6:00 PM, Dr. Gallo, in his hotel room, was putting on a dinner jacket. He liked and took pride in being punctual. He picked up his overcoat and carried it to the hotel lobby, where Aaron and Beth were waiting. For the first time, they were not arguing. Dr. Gallo jokingly remarked, "Is there something wrong? You are not arguing with each other."

Aaron glanced at Beth, who replied, "Actually, Dr. Gallo, we missed you, and we are both very glad you're back."

Looking uncomfortable at her words and stroking his hair back, Aaron added, "Yes, but don't tell any of our friends we told you this. You know that we missed you."

Dr. Gallo smiled at them and replied, "Actually, truth be told, I also missed you both, and please don't tell this to any of my friends back at the university." Both Aaron and Beth chuckled, and Aaron said, "Our secret. So, where are we going to eat?"

"Well, I promised you some fine French cuisine," and patting his coat and then checking his back pocket, he said, "Oh, I must have forgotten my wallet in the coat I was wearing on the flight. Let me go back to my room, get it, and I'll be right back. You are going to love this café. It overlooks the Seine River."

He turned and decided to run up the stairs. It was only two flights. When he unlocked his hotel room and stepped in, he saw an intruder by an open window. No doubt about it, that was the entry point, Gallo thought. The intruder was not a very large man but had a stocky body build and had his back to him. He was talking to someone on his phone while carrying the metal object found with the scrolls in his other hand. When the intruder heard the door open, he was clearly startled.

Gallo rushed at him, tackling the intruder and the nearby end table and lamp to the floor. Gallo heard a grunt from the intruder as if the fall had taken his breath away. With the fall, both the metal object and the intruder's phone were knocked loose from his hands, and both lay on the floor. The intruder seemed to panic and started to hit the floor next to him with open palms, searching for his phone and the metal object. Unsuccessful in finding either one, he stood up from the floor and ran, jumping out of the open window, which led to a fire escape.

Gallo heard a thud and another grunt coming from the window and then heard footsteps running away. He went to the opened window and could see only the dark alley below and behind his hotel. Glancing around the room, he noted nothing else disturbed except his carry-on luggage. The suitcase was open with the scrolls still in their place. Only the metal object had been removed, and now it lay on the floor not far from the intruder's phone. He didn't touch anything.

He called downstairs for security to report a break-in into his hotel room. He glanced at the intruder's phone, and it had a phone number still showing. Recognizing it as a New York City number by its area code, he felt a chill run down his spine. His students came up to his room with the hotel security guard, a middle-aged man who once served in the French army.

Shortly thereafter, Inspector Henri Allard arrived. He had been having dinner at a nearby café and decided to walk over to the hotel and review the break-in. Inspector Allard was a thirty-year veteran in the police force and enjoyed his work. He had a touch of grey at his temples and a full head of hair. He was dressed in a dark, double-vested pinstripe suit, a white shirt with a thin dark tie, and a Dior Homme trench coat that Gallo recognized from his window shopping on his last visit to Paris. The Inspector appeared to be a regular jogger or at least a frequent gym attendee, radiating confidence as he approached Gallo and the crime scene.

"Good evening, Dr. Gallo," Inspector Allard said, "I was informed by the front desk clerk you are a Jesuit priest here for a conference? But you are not dressed like a priest." He did not wait for an answer and walked over to the opened window, fallen table, and lamp. Next to the lamp lay the metal object and the intruder's phone. The Inspector donned some cotton gloves he removed from his trench coat pocket, picking up the phone to examine it before placing it into an evidence bag. He then texted something on his phone before turning his attention to the metal object.

Gallo said, "That metal object, Inspector, was loaned and entrusted to me by the government of Jordan and I was planning to carry it back to my laboratory at Georgetown University to further study it. I have papers substantiating that if you wish to see them."

The Inspector, a devoted Catholic, said, "We need to dust it for prints. It looks like a bad blade but with no sharp edges and no sharp tip. Hmm, I find this very interesting."

Looking worried and horrified about the idea of losing sight of the blade, he asked the Inspector if it could be dusted for prints in his hotel room.

The Inspector, sensing Gallo's worries, remained professional yet respectful of Gallo's situation and said, "I think there is a forensic team nearby, and I can ask them to come by and dust for prints. Let me call them. I must be getting into, as you say, into the Christmas spirit," he said, smiling to himself as he made a call on his phone.

Turning his attention to his students, Gallo walked to them and said, "I'm sorry about this, and it looks like I'm going to be here longer than any of us expected."

Aaron said, "No worries, we can wait."

"No, no, no, I have reservations at this café. You and Beth go on ahead and have yourselves a nice dinner. Mention to the owner that you are my students, and they will treat you very well. I've been eating there for years, and everything on the menu is great. I know I've ordered it all. Here, take my credit card; they know it all too well."

Beth said, "That's very nice of you, Dr. Gallo, but we can wait."

Just then, Inspector Allard said to Gallo, "They will be here within the hour." Relieved, Gallo said, "There, you see, I'll meet you there as soon as we are finished here."

Aaron and Beth reluctantly left the hotel room. The Inspector walked over to Gallo and asked if anything else might have been stolen. Gallo paused, took another look around the room, and said, "No, not that I can see."

Then, taking a pause to ponder the situation, Inspector Allard said, "Then, it would seem, other than the break-in, there was no other crime committed? We take hotel room break-ins very seriously… bad for tourism."

Gallo, still gazing at the metal object and then turning his attention to Inspector Allard, said, "I noticed a New York City phone number on the intruder's phone. He was talking to someone when I interrupted him."

"Yes, one of my men is tracing that number now. I just texted the number to him," the Inspector said and added, "What is this metal object? Why would the intruder want it?

Gallo explained how it came to be under his possession, and when he finished, the crime scene squad entered the room and started checking the metal object for prints.

Looking at his watch, Inspector Allard said, "Dr. Gallo, or should I call you Father Gallo? It shouldn't be long now. I know this team. They are the best we have in Paris."

After about thirty minutes and thoroughly looking at the entire blade, the team leader walked to the Inspector and said, "There were no prints detected. It was entirely clean."

At that moment, the Inspector received a text message, pausing to read it. He thanked the crime scene team for their diligence, and they all left. Gallo, overhearing the report of no prints on the metal object, approached the Inspector with an incredulous look. "That's impossible; several people have handled it, including myself, just this afternoon. How can that be?" Gallo exclaimed in surprise.

Not offering any explanation for the absence of fingerprints, the Inspector looked up from his phone at Gallo and said, "I just received a text telling me that the intruder was on the phone with someone at the Headquarters of the Society of Angels in New York City. I'm very familiar with this Society. My wife gives a modest donation to them every year. They have an office here, in the old part of Paris in fact not far from this hotel. They hold yearly fundraisers. A very nice event attended by some of the wealthiest residents living in Paris. Well, Dr. Gallo, you may keep the metal object in your possession. It has no use to us, but at least we have the intruder's phone."

Relieved, Gallo replied, "Thank you, Inspector, and thank you for letting me know the phone number's origin. I might just pay them a visit when I return to the States."

The Inspector, again looking around the room and outside the opened window, turned to Gallo and said, "You may want to close the window. I think it might rain tonight as it's getting colder. I think we have all we need and perhaps the intruder's phone will have some prints and some clues as to why he was in your room to begin with. Oh, I will need some contact information from you in case something comes up that might concern you." Handing Gallo his card, "Here is one of my cards, should you have any more problems!"

"Yes, of course. I'll let your office know how to contact me first thing tomorrow morning. Inspector Allard, thank you for your understanding." Replied Gallo.

The Inspector sighed and muttered, "No prints on a strange metal object and the Society of Angels…Hmm, I find this very interesting," and continued to walk out the hotel door.

Gallo walked to the open window, closed it, and then picked up the metal object. He placed it underneath his shirt between his belt and the small of his back and then left his room headed to the café where his students were and no doubt confused about what had just happened.

# Chapter 6

The next day was the last day of the conference, and Gallo delivered his talk as scheduled. He started his talk with a review of the research previously done by another Jesuit priest, Jose O'Callaghan Mendoza, who identified evidence of the New Testament in one of the Dead Sea Scrolls found in Cave 7. Though initially dismissed by scholars, further analysis eventually confirmed his groundbreaking theory. Gallo proposed that additional evidence of the New Testament could be found in other similar scrolls and presented his findings. It was well received and all knew much more work was needed to confirm his findings. Notably, he did not mention his new acquisition, the Book of Enoch, to anyone at the conference, and he had instructed his students to remain equally discreet.

At noon, during the lunch break, Gallo turned to Aaron and Beth and asked, "How would you like to walk the streets of Paris and visit the Eifel Tower and see Monet's Water Lilies at the Musee de l'Orangerie? We leave tomorrow morning. This is our last day in Paris. What do you think?" Beth immediately jumped up with joy, her face lighting up as she said, "Count me in!"

Aaron, equally excited, nodded, "Our last day in Paris, definitely count me in too!"

As they strolled out of the Latin Quarter of Paris, where the Sorbonne is located, Gallo noticed a building that was not far from their hotel. It had a large bronze plaque on its front door. There was a winged angel with its head bowed, hands resting on the hilt of an upright sword. Surrounding the image were the words Société des Anges.

Society of Angels. Part of Gallo wanted to go and enter that building and learn more about them. His walking pace slowed, and his attention was directed to the Society's building when Aaron looked at him and asked, "Is everything alright, Dr. Gallo?"

Gallo hesitated and, feeling as if he were awakened from a trance, said, "Uh, yes, Aaron and Beth, this is a time to build good memories."

They continued their walk, and Gallo hailed a taxi to take them to the Eiffel Tower. The three of them wandered the streets of Paris, taking in the wonderful smells of the nearby restaurants, the Christmas lights, the music played by the stores still open that evening, and finally ending their day by the Seine River at a quaint café sipping delicious French wine.

All in all, it was a memorable day in Paris for all three of them. All the while, Gallo kept the metal object hidden on him while the scrolls remained safely stored in the hotel's secure vault.

# Chapter 7

The return flight to DC was uneventful other than convincing the security at the airport that the metal piece in Gallo's carry-on was not a weapon. He purposely wore his priest collar and carried his Georgetown University identification badge to further make a compelling argument that he was not a terrorist. Upon arrival at DC, he told his students to take the rest of the weekend off and that he would meet them Monday morning in the lab.

Both students were in the lab early Monday morning to discuss the next steps for their research projects. Gallo entered, carrying the scrolls carefully in his arms, and placed them gently on the nearby lab bench. "Good morning, Aaron and Beth. I believe we have an important and unique opportunity before us. And that would be to start working on the translation of these scrolls.

Turning to Aaron, Gallo asked, "How's your Hebrew?"

Excited at the prospect of translating the entire Book of Enoch, Aaron said, "Pretty good, sir." "Beth, how is your Hebrew?" Gallo asked Beth.

Beth responded, "Probably not as good as Aaron's, but I like the challenge. When can we start?"

With a look of satisfaction, Gallo clasped his hands together, rubbed them in anticipation, and said, "Good! Let's get started. The Book of Enoch can be divided into three sections; each of us will take one section, and the plan is we translate in the morning, and in the afternoon, we review our findings and check each other's work for errors. How does that sound to everyone?"

Aaron and Beth exchanged enthusiastic smiles. "Can we start now?" Beth asked eagerly.

Gallo opened a desk drawer, pulled out a box of cotton gloves and three magnifying glasses, and handed them to each.

Aaron, glancing around, asked, "Where is the metal object?"

"I put that in a safe location, so let's not worry about it now," said Gallo, looking a little somber, remembering the intruder in his Paris hotel room.

Gallo carefully divided the scrolls into three sections, then turned back to his students. "These are the three books of Enoch that are agreed upon by scholars." He continued, "I will start on the first book, Aaron, you have the second book and Beth the third book." Gallo continued, "When I first reviewed the Book of Enoch, written in an ancient Ethiopian dialect There were missing parts, I felt. This scroll is much more complete. It has added additional text not present in the Ethiopian scrolls."

It was late morning, and each of them was studiously translating the scrolls when Marge appeared at the lab door. "Dr. Gallo, you have a long-distance phone call from a man calling himself Inspector Allard from Paris. Sounds important, so I thought I would tell you myself in person."

"Inspector Allard," Gallo repeated, slightly puzzled. "Yes, Marge, can you transfer him to this phone in our lab?"

As the phone buzzed, Gallo picked it up and said, "This is Dr. Gallo."

He heard the Inspector's voice, "We found the man who broke into your hotel room and identified him by his fingerprints on the phone he was carrying. He was a common thief, his name was Hugo Fontaine, unfortunately, he was found dead, drowned in the river Seine. The only thing in his possession was a business card for the local chapter of the Society of Angels here in Paris." He paused then he said, "I called you in case you try to contact the Society of Angels in New York. There are many reasons why this common thief would be found dead, and perhaps he was stealing only to gain money to donate to his favorite charity or perhaps not. It may be coincidental that the only phone number the thief had in his phone was that of Society's headquarters in New York and that he also had a business card from the same society here in Paris. And it may also be a coincidence that the time of his death is most likely the same night he escaped from your hotel room. Hmm, I find that to be strange; be careful, Dr. Gallo." "Thank you, Inspector," Gallo said before hanging up.

Intrigued more than alarmed, Gallo looked up at his students. "That was Inspector Allard from Paris." He recounted what the Inspector reported to him and then asked, "Why would a philanthropic society have an interest in a Dead Sea Scroll or an ancient artifact?" "Perhaps they are collectors," said Beth, adjusting her chair."

"Or," Aaron chimed in with a grin, "Maybe this blade has magical powers, and they are tired of asking for donations and just want to rule the world," said Aaron jokingly.

"Really, Aaron, said Gallo, smiling with a sense of relief but still intrigued, "And you want to be the ethicist of this group? Okay, which one of you wants to go to New York with me tomorrow and pay a visit to the Society of Angels? One of you has to stay in the lab in my absence."

"I'll stay," said Aaron. "I'd like to continue with my translation of the scrolls."

Gallo, rising to his feet and picking up the phone, said, "I'll call the Society of Angels. Headquarters now for a meeting tomorrow, stating we have a very important project that cannot wait, and we would like to discuss research funding in person. We can take an early train and get back by tomorrow evening. Are you okay with that, Beth?"

"I'm all in," replied Beth with a determined look.

# Chapter 8

When they arrived at the busy New York train station, Gallo and Beth took a taxi to Stone Street near the old Goldman Sachs building on Broad Street. It was the first headquarters for Goldman Sachs before moving to a new tower. The original building was built on the first paved road in New York City on the original 17th-century cobblestones, which were preserved as the first floor of the lobby. Although Goldman Sachs headquarters had moved to their own tower, the older building was still used for some business transactions. Part of the building was rented to the Society of Angels as a tax write-off for Goldman Sachs.

Outside the entrance a bronze plaque showed an angel holding a sword pointing down, surrounded by the words "Society of Angels." It was the same design Gallo saw on the plaque at the Society's Paris building. It didn't look out of place but there were few markings on the building identifying it as the Society of Angels Headquarters.

They were not advertising themselves and their location. Perhaps to avoid unwanted random guests, Gallo thought to himself. As they walked through the entry door, they found a large, empty lobby with a large desk and no other piece of furniture. They were shocked to see that even there was no place to sit. The walls were made of beautiful burled mahogany wood. A young woman dressed in an expensive-looking outfit sat behind a desk, politely greeted them, and asked how she could help them.

"We have an appointment with your director about possible funding for a new and exciting project. My name is Dr. Gallo from Georgetown University, and this is my assistant, Beth O'Conner," said Gallo.

Without any outward emotion, the young lady behind the desk said, "Yes, the director is expecting you. You may take the elevators to your right and go to the top floor. Someone there will greet you and show you the way."

"Thank you," said Gallo as he and Beth walked over to the elevators. Gallo found it strange that there was no one else around in such a big lobby, no other visitors or staff.

Upon arrival to the top floor, the elevator doors opened, and there stood a tall man in a black suit who looked more like a bodyguard than a guide. He politely said hello and asked them to follow him. Oddly, there was only one door at the end of a long hallway with no identifying marks. Again, the walls were lined with burled wood with an arching ceiling that instantly gave Gallo the feel of entering a Gothic Church.

As they entered the director's office, there was only a large desk with a transparent top with blinking lights that could be seen under the surface. It was no more than three inches thick with black siding and dark tapering glass-like legs. The floor was made of yellow pine wood in excellent condition covered by an antique Persian rug. To their utmost surprise, there were no chairs for the attendees, and they were left standing in that magnificent room. The wooden walls had carvings that seemed to tell a story. They looked like biblical figures by the robes they wore, but the figures closer to the door were more modern in appearance.

Gallo did not get the time to examine the carvings when a sliding door opened behind the desk, and a tall man with graying hair stepped out. His suit was perfectly tailored, and his deep voice was calm as he greeted them, "Good morning, Dr. Gallo and Ms. O'Conner. I'm Director Kobel Price.

"Thank you for meeting us on such short notice, Director Price," Gallo said, his voice filled with gratefulness.

"Dr. Gallo, it was very good to hear from you. I'm a big fan of your work especially your work on the Dead Sea Scrolls," the man replied in a graceful manner.

"Thank you, that is exactly why we are here. Ms. O'Conner is studying the Dead Sea Scrolls and their relationship to the origin of ethics, her thesis," as Gallo said, he nodded towards Beth.

"Please to meet you Ms. O'Conner," Price said.

Beth, clearly impressed, blurted out, "What a beautiful suit. Is that wool and cashmere?"

Gallo looked a little startled at what he had just heard but kept his composure. "Vicuna," Price corrected.

"Oh, sorry, sir. I didn't mean to be so presumptuous and I'm embarrassed. My mother is a seamstress, and every opportunity she had, she made a point of teaching me about the different fabrics and their uses." Beth felt a little embarrassed and apologized instantly.

"Well, thank you for asking. It is seldom these days that I receive a compliment from such a young lady." Price smiled.

"Ahh, well, yes, Director, if I may get to our purpose for this visit. I have come into possession of a newly found scroll that is in pristine condition and written in the original Hebrew. The scroll is the Book of Enoch." Gallo quickly redirected the conversation.

"Please tell me more, Dr. Gallo," Price inquired.

"I would like to get funding to get an accurate date of its writing and also hire a linguistic expert in the field of Biblical Hebrew. My Hebrew is good, but I always feel better when someone else confirms my findings," Gallo said with utter humility in his tone.

"And these scrolls, what else was found with them?" Price asked.

"I'm not sure I know what you mean," replied Gallo.

Gallo hesitated, surprised by the question, "I understand a metal object was also found in the vase," said the Director.

Gallo, with a surprised look, "How could you possibly know?"

"Oh, Dr. Gallo, we have offices all over the world, and we do thorough background checks on everyone who requests funding," said Price. He then walked behind his desk and waved his hand over it. A thin transparent screen rolled up from the desk. Gallo could see through the transparent screen and saw a picture of himself with what appeared to be writings, most likely his biography. "You see, we have already done some research on you and your two graduate students. I'm very impressed with your background and your work." "However," looking at Beth, "We missed the information about your mother and your keen interest and understanding of haberdashery," he added.

Beth looked down and was clearly embarrassed.

Looking at Gallo, the director continued, "But to answer your question as to how I know about the metal object, your friend Professor Amer Hassan at the University of Jordan told one of our agents about this find. He was also seeking funds to investigate the age of the vase, which is still in his possession. So, you see I'm very glad to support your research. You will need to fill out a grant request, a mere formality for you, and then you must submit it to our Grant Office for their review." He then waved his hand over the screen monitor, and it sleekly retreated into the desk. "But I cannot imagine any foreseeable obstacle to your request. The receptionist downstairs will hand you the grant application package as you leave."

"Well, that's very kind of you." We won't take up any more of your time," said Gallo, still trying to comprehend how the Director knew so much about him, his friend Amer, his students, and his project. For Gallo, it was a moment of shock, and he was completely taken aback by it, and he was trying to make sense of everything in his mind.

Looking at his pocket watch, the Director said, "Yes, I actually have a very busy schedule this morning, but I did wanted to meet you. Oh, Dr. Gallo, do you still have that metal object?" Looking puzzled and wanting to show the Director respect for granting him his time on such short notice, he replied, "Why yes... We have it in a safe place."

"That is wise. Good day." The Director gave the nod and then turned, walking toward his desk as the sliding door behind it opened without even the faintest sound of a motor. It closed just as silently behind him as he disappeared into the dark room beyond.

Gallo and Beth were escorted out of his office, and as they passed the receptionist's desk, she handed Gallo a brown package, saying to him, "You will find everything you need in this package," she said politely.

The train ride back to D.C. was quiet. Gallo and Beth sat across from each other, deep in thought. Finally, they looked at each other and simultaneously said, "He knew."

Gallo, looking puzzled, "But how could he have known so much?" For a person like Gallo, it was unusual to be out of the answers.

Frowning, Beth said, "And how can someone working for a charity and philanthropic organization afford such an expensive suit? Vicuna... Wow."

"When we get back home, I plan to call my friend in Jordan," Gallo said, his thoughts still swirling around his mind.

Beth nodded and said, "He made me feel very nervous, as though he could see through me, and that's despite his deep, calming voice and kind face."

When they arrived in D.C., the air between them was still heavy with questions, as if both were still trying to process their meeting. They said "Good Night" to each other and agreed to meet tomorrow morning at Dr. Gallo's lab.

When Gallo reached his apartment, it was late; he sat for a while, took in a deep breath, and decided to wait for a more appropriate time to call his friend, Amer, at the University. It already had been a long, strange day, and he couldn't shake the uneasy feeling that followed him into his restless sleep.

# Chapter 9

Gallo arrived early the next day, and upon entering the department, he saw Marge, who liked to have an early start and was usually in the office before anyone else. "Good morning", he greeted her. "Marge, it's 7:30 in the morning here, which means it should be 2:30 P.M. in Amman, Jordan. Do you remember Professor Hassan? He was here last year discussing some of his research with the members of our department," he continued.

"Yes, I remember him very well. He was so polite and sophisticated. I liked him," said Marge with a smile.

"I'll call him right away; I kept all his information," she added, whispering to herself, "Yes, all of it."

"Great, thank you. I'll be in my office," Gallo continued, walking to his office with a brief pause at Professor Jack Murphy's office door to greet his old friend before heading into his own office.

As he sat down in his chair, his phone rang. It was Marge who told him that Professor Hassan had been missing for the last five days and that his family was very worried about him and his whereabouts. Gallo was stunned and didn't know how to respond. He heard Marge's voice over the phone asking him if he was still on the line, and finally, after a brief pause of silence, he responded and asked Marge to please let the Professor's secretary know that he would like to be kept updated on his friend's status. He wasn't sure what to think about his friend being missing, the men in suites going to the farmhouse of the boy who found the scrolls, the break-in at his hotel room in Paris, and how, if at all, these events were connected to the Society of Angels. He decided to bury himself in his research for the day, focusing on translating the scrolls.

Gallo's lab served both as a classroom and a research area. There were multiple reference books laid out on the long lab tables and pictures on the walls of the known twelve caves containing the Dead Sea Scroll alongside maps of their locations. Next to these pictures, there were replicas of old paintings depicting some of the events described in the Dead Sea Scrolls.

After a long day of pouring over the scrolls and slowly translating them, Beth pulled down her mask and asked with curiosity, "Who were the Nephilim? Enoch described them as the children of angels and human women."

Well, yes!" Gallo responded, "They were the offspring of the Watchers, two hundred angels overseeing humanity's role on this earth. Their name, Nephilim in Hebrew, means fallen ones. They were described as superhuman, immortals, and by others as giants. Their eyes were said to have a silvery glow in the darkness. I think the word giant should not be taken literally but rather as a reference to their supernatural abilities. When the first cave was found, there were twenty-one scrolls found. One was the Book of War. In it, it tells the story of a battle between the Sons of Light against the Sons of Darkness. They go into battle with each side having angels and supernatural beings fighting with them..." He continued after a breathing pause, "I believe these supernatural beings were the children of the angels, the Nephilim. We don't know what exactly became of these children and why they were battling each other. They are not mentioned in any other book other than the Book of Enoch. What makes these scrolls so interesting and so important is that they are written in Hebrew, which was thought of as the language of Enoch. This may very well be his original text written by him. The only other translation is in an Ethiopian dialect, which has omissions." Gallo finished his sentence as he looked into the space, getting lost in his thought process.

Beth, intrigued, asked, "So we may actually find out what happened to them? Could it be revealed in this more complete text? But I thought there was a Book of Giants, and they were the Nephilim?" Smiling at Beth and surprised that she knew of the Book of Giants, Gallo looked at both Aaron and Beth and replied, "Yes, in the early translation of the Book of Giants, what little remains of it, mentioned the Nephilim and incorrectly labeled them as giants; because the word for Nephilim was misinterpreted. That Hebrew word that was misinterpreted could be translated as abortion or animal, not giants. I believe these giants, as described in The Book of Giants, were not Nephilim but perhaps the result of some type of experiment gone awry. Perhaps performed by the Nephilim on various animals. I don't know what became of these giants," he then looked into the space and started, after a brief pause, "One, named Og, managed to escape the great deluge and was reported to have lived five thousand years; however, we do not know what happened to him. The giants were supposed to be immortal. They were described as beastly and destructive, and I pray the four angels sent by God to deal with these giants, Raphael, Michael, Gabriel, and Israel, managed to be rid of them."

Aaron, who had been listening intently, chimed in, "Wow, this is real supernatural sci-fi stuff. Pretty cool. Maybe Big Foot and the Yeti are some of the giants that remain on Earth."

Gallo gave Aaron a disapproving look, "Let's not get carried away with our imagination."

"Yeah, so far, I've not come across anything that mentions the Nephilim for my part," said Aaron.

"Well, we've just translated about 15% of the text. It's getting late; it's almost 6:00 pm, and we should get some rest and agree to restart early tomorrow morning," said Gallo as he glanced at the clock.

Carefully, Gallo gathered their scrolls using acid-free cotton gloves that he required Aaron and Beth to use as well as to wear a mask while being near the scrolls so as not to contaminate them or, worse, breathe in ancient spores. He was not tired at all and was still thinking about how the Society of Angels was involved, if at all. He went to his office with the scrolls and put them into a safe under his desk. As to the metal object, he had placed it in a different safe in a nearby office that was currently not in use. The office belongs to his former mentor, Dr. Medina, who was on a sabbatical in Rome.

As Gallo sat down, he picked up the package given to him at the office of the Society of Angels the day before, but it seemed like a very long time ago. From his office window, he could see the Chesapeake and Ohio Canal and some joggers on the nearby trail. He enjoyed his early morning runs, but in this last week, he was so preoccupied with recent events that he unknowingly abandoned his routine. When he opened the package, he thought to himself he really had no intention of pursuing a grant from the Society of Angels, or at least not until he knew more about them. To his surprise, inside the package was not just an application for a grant but also a piece of paper with a handwritten note saying call me with a phone number and no signature. This intrigued his mind, and he instantly made a phone call. Although it was closer to 7:00 P.M., he didn't think twice and dialed the number. The number had a New York City area code, but there was no answer. He didn't feel comfortable leaving a voicemail, so he hung up and thought perhaps he would try calling it again in the morning.

He tucked the piece of paper with the phone number into his coat pocket and left the grant application untouched. He then stepped out and locked his office. Other than a few graduate students, he did not see anyone else in the building. As he walked to the parking lot, he thought of his friend in Jordan and decided that he would try calling him again in the morning.

On his walk home, he felt as though he was being watched but didn't want to give too much thought to it and tried not to dwell on it.

He once again had another restless night.

# Chapter 10

## Day 9

Upon arriving at his office, Dr. Gallo found a note on his desk. It read, *"Sorry I missed your call last night; call me."* He rushed out, calling to his secretary, "Marge, have you seen anyone enter my office this morning?"

Without looking up from her typing, she replied, "No."

He returned to his desk and dialed the number on the note. This time, the phone barely rang once before he heard a woman's voice with what sounded like a French accent. She said, "Dr. Gallo, meet me tonight, 8:30 at the corner of Blagden Alley. I will explain everything you need to know then." She hung up abruptly, and when he tried to call back, he was greeted by a recording informing him that the number was no longer in service.

Puzzled but intrigued, he made his way to the lab, where he found Aaron and Beth involved in a spirited debate about the origins of ethics. Beth was arguing that the origins of all ethical behavior could be traced to the influence of the great religions of the world, and Aaron countered that there is no such thing as a tabula rasa, and the great religions have only reinforced our innate sense of morality.

Gallo couldn't help but smile. "As much as I want to become a part of this conversation," he continued, "The translation of the scrolls must take priority."

"Round two later," said Beth, playfully nudging Aaron, who just silently mouthed, "You're on," while pointing his finger at her.

"Alright, everyone, mask up, put on your gloves, and head to your corners. Let's get started!" Gallo is acting like a referee.

With a few groans of objection, Aaron and Beth moved toward their stations, uncovered the scrolls, and continued their translations. Both Aaron and Beth had a working knowledge of modern-day Hebrew, but ancient Hebrew, better known as Biblical Hebrew, had some slight variations in interpretation, so both were careful to reference all their translations. The day passed uneventfully, aside from a brief lunch break they each took separately. By late afternoon, their reviews of the translations revealed nothing new. It was 5:30 P.M. when Gallo called it a day, and he went back to his office to consolidate the day's findings. He realized he forgot to call his friend in Jordan and made a mental note to call him tomorrow. "Ahh," whispering to himself, "I will call him tomorrow."

The meeting time was approaching, and he decided to take a taxi rather than the Metro, which he preferred, which is nonexistent in Georgetown. He directed the cab driver to 9th Street NW and M Street, planning to walk the final stretch to Blagden Alley. Once, it was described as a ruined area or residential slum with underground raves is now rejuvenated and has transformed in recent years. The old stables and shops were replaced by a Philadelphia-based coffee shop at one corner, and not far from it, a Michelin-starred restaurant. Artists and young creatives had brought new life to the area, making it a thriving hub of culture and renewal. Tonight, however, the alleyway was dark, and the corner coffee shop was closed. It was indeed an odd sight.

It was dark, and a light snow began to fall. As Dr. Gallo approached the corner of the Cathedral of Saint Matthew, he could see the silhouette of a thin, tall woman standing. She turned to him, and he could see the face of an attractive woman with dark hair, fair skin, and high cheekbones speaking to him in a French accent and said, "Good evening, Dr. Gallo." Her voice was soft but was throwing a sense of urgency.

Dr. Gallo replied cautiously, "Good evening. To whom am I addressing?"

"Dr. Gallo, I'm here to tell you that you are in grave danger as long as you have God's talisman." The woman replied, her tone alarming.

"God's talisman? I am not sure I understand. What is God's talisman?" Dr. Gallo replied, perplexed.

Her gaze was intense, and her voice took on a tone of deep concern. "The metal object found with the Hebrew Book of Enoch is what I speak of. It carries great powers. Powers that can lead to the destruction of civilization as you know it."

Still puzzled, Gallo said, "I still don't understand. What powers?"

She leaned closer and said, "Destroy it or forever keep it hidden from public view." And with that, she retreated into the darkness of the alley, and for a brief moment, her eyes revealed a soft silvery glow that soon disappeared. As Gallo moved toward her, calling out, "Wait! I still have many more questions." But her voice echoed distantly, "Do not try to follow me, Dr. Gallo."

Muttering to himself he said slowly, "What happen to telling me everything I need t know?"

He stood there, shaken and confused, wondering how she had vanished so quickly. And what type of power was she speaking about? It's just a very hard and light-weight piece of metal, he thought to himself.

Frustration simmered within him as he walked away; he was very dissatisfied with the meeting. "Perhaps," he thought, the answers lie in the scrolls. If they hold any hint of this so-called talisman's power, their translation has become far more urgent.

# Chapter 11

## Day 10

The next morning, when he walked into the Department, Marge spotted him, calling out, "Dr Gallo, they found Professor Hassan… He is in the hospital, and only immediate family is allowed to visit. But he specifically requested to speak with you in person." There is a flight to Amman tomorrow afternoon. Shall I book it?"

Sighing with a new surge of inspiration, he responded, "Your intuitive help is incredible. Yes, please book it."

He then walked into his lab, only to find Aaron and Beth with excited faces, smiling and bursting to tell him of their findings. Aaron started with Enoch's story of the two hundred Watchers and how their children born of human women appeared to be even more powerful than their angel fathers and how Azazel, the leader of the Watchers, was in disagreement with his second in command, Kokbel also called Kakabel.

Then, Aaron continued, "Azazel believed their children should transform the earth into their own likeness, whereas Kokbel believed they should return to God and ask for his forgiveness and let humans choose their own destiny or as God wills it. They chose to side with humans and went to war against each other, which would explain the Book of War…" He continued after a pause, "How both the Sons of Light and Sons of Darkness fought against each other and both with angels and supernatural beings alongside them. You were right, Dr. Gallo; these supernatural beings are the children of the angels, the Nephilim." When he finished his sentence, his face was glowing with a sense of pride in their work.

Beth excitedly added, "Enoch then tells us that God gave him the talisman that when touched by a Nephilim, he or she would hear

God's voice calling for their return. Enoch also speaks of the ring's power. If placed on the talisman resting on the hilt, it would send God's call to all Nephilim and all angelic beings within seventy-seven cubits to return to him…" After a pause, she continued, "Seventy-seven cubits, that's an odd number."

"But there is more," Beth continued, "Enoch used the Talisman and the ring when he was threatened by a Nephilim. He placed the ring on the hilt of the Talisman and not just the Nephilim was vanquished but also two of God's angels sent to protect him."

Then Aaron jumped and continued explaining their findings, "That if the ring was left on the talisman, every seven days, the range of the talisman's power would extend seven times more until God could be heard by them all over the world."

Beth asked, "So, what is it about the number seven?"

Gallo, recalling his reading of numerology and the meaning of certain numbers in the Bible, said, "Seventy-seven is how many times Jesus told Peter to forgive his brother, and repeating sevens is in reference to angels and when they are called upon to restore order." He then started strolling, "Biblical numerology was popular among kabbalists and Jewish mystics and is largely not taken seriously by most scholars today. And a cubit?" He took a pause, then continued, "It's an ancient unit of length based on the length from the elbow to the tip of the middle finger or about one and a half feet long, which would make the range of God's word to be heard about a 115-foot radius."

Beth continued, "What's more, Enoch apparently buried the ring near the scrolls, fearing the combined power of talisman and ring."

Gallo's eyes lit up. "The ring must still be in the cave! All the more reason to go visit my friend Professor Hassan in Amman," he continued, "This could be why Professor Hassan urgently wants to see me. He must know something critical."

Aaron, sensing both the danger and adventure, asked, "Wait, Dr. Gallo, you are going back to Jordan to look for this ring? Don't you think it might be dangerous? Can I come?"

Beth, not wanting to be left behind, said loudly, "I think I should go too."

Glancing seriously at his team, he responded, "No, no, this is something that I and I alone must do. I didn't mention it, but I had a strange encounter last night with a woman who warned me that talisman has powers—enough to potentially destroy our civilization. I don't fully understand that warning, but I will. I plan to move the talisman to a more secure location later tonight and I don't want either of you near here. Understand?

He looked pointedly at Aaron, then at Beth. "I need to hear you say it."

With reluctant nods, they both responded, "Understood."

That evening, by 8:00 pm, the halls were silent, and an occasional door slamming could be heard. Gallo, in his office, decided to move the talisman to another location but still somewhere inside the building. He thought of the janitor's closet on the same floor. It contained a small closet with a lock. A secure and unsuspecting place. Oddly, years earlier, a metal closet was installed in order to safeguard toiletries that were being stolen during the COVID years of shortages and isolation.

The closet was no longer in use, and he had managed to get a key to the lock; in fact, he now owned the only existing key to this closet. He went to Professor Medina's office to retrieve the talisman, as it was now called. The hallways were no longer well-lit, but he felt safe.

Upon reaching the office where the talisman was located, he methodically opened the safe and removed the talisman. He sat in Professor Medina's chair for a while to examine this object, which had now become a central figure in his research. He noticed what could be a handle, and as part of the hub, there was a circular indentation where he imagined the ring would lay to weaponize it.

He again was amazed as to how light it felt in his hands and how tough it was against a diamond blade. This was truly God's talisman, forged by God for only one purpose: to capture the remaining Nephilim. A powerful weapon indeed. But how could it destroy civilization as we know it? He got up from the chair, stepped into the dark hallway, and started walking to the janitor's room when he heard a voice saying, "Stop."

Turning, he saw a pair of silvery eyes gleaming from a dark corner. His heart raced as he recognized the figure, a Nephilim. Before he could make his next move, he was tackled to the floor by a powerful figure in a hooded robe, wearing gloves and a ski mask. The Nephilim moved swiftly and gracefully as he pounced on him. Gallo fell hard to the floor, the impact knocking the breath from his lungs as pain shot through his shoulder. The Nephilim pinned him down; its grip was tight.

Gallo, still holding on to the talisman with his right hand, felt the Nephilim's vice-like grip on his wrist. His hand and wrist were rapidly becoming numb and painful. The Nephilim was over him, straddling his torso, and it was still dark enough that Gallo could see the silvery eyes focused on him and then turning their attention to the talisman. He was a powerful being who then began to pry open his hand that held the talisman with his gloved hand.

Then, suddenly, the lights flooded the hallway. Aaron and Beth had arrived, flipping the switch after hearing muffled shouts. The Nephilim turned toward Aaron and Beth, momentarily loosening its grip on Gallo. Seizing the chance, Gallo used his free hand to pull back the creature's sleeve, exposing its forearm, and quickly pressed the talisman against it. He moved his right wrist, allowing the talisman to touch the Nephilim's bared forearm. Upon the talisman touching the exposed forearm, there was a high-pitched sound that came and went, and he witnessed the Nephilim burst into a thousand specks of bright white lights that glowed for an instant and rapidly faded. All that was left were the Nephilim's robe, gloves, and mask that rested on him.

Gallo lay gasping while Aaron and Beth stood motionless at the end of the hallway, their faces frozen in shock. Finally lifting his head, he managed a weak smile in gratitude for their intervention. But then, his voice shifted to a stern tone as he demanded, "What are you doing here?"

Beth, still in a state of disbelief, said, "We were thinking, well, we were trying to help. We came up with a number of very good places to hide the talisman, and all these places are around the campus, so we could keep an eye out for any prowlers, and we wanted to share our ideas with you. But… But what just happened?"

Aaron, still stunned, could only say, "Creepy!"

Gallo said with a sense of wonder, "I think we just heard God's calling." "Woah," Aaron let out.

"So, did we just witness a Nephilim return to God?" asked Beth.

"I do believe that is exactly what we saw, but I still don't understand how this talisman threatens our civilization. It's more of a threat to the Nephilim. Or perhaps to all angels on earth if the story about the ring is true." Gallo nodded slowly.

He then turned his attention to Aaron and Beth and instructed them to return to their dorms and that he would meet them tomorrow morning in the lab before he would leave for Amman. He further stressed that not a word to anyone about what they saw here tonight and said, "Promise me. Promise me." His voice softened.

Aaron and Beth, in disbelief and stunned, looked at each other, and then both nodded yes to him.

Gallo picked up the talisman and exited through the back door while Aaron and Beth left through the front, making their way to their respective dorms. As they walked, an unusual fatigue overcame them both, as if the evening's events had drained them. Each reached their room and collapsed into bed, falling into a heavy, unyielding sleep.

That night, they both shared the same dream. They found themselves working alone in the lab, translating the scrolls when the lab became dark. First, a single pair of silvery eyes was staring at them from a distance, and then they were suddenly surrounded by many pairs of silvery eyes. They heard a distant voice asking them to reveal the location of the talisman, for it belonged to them. It is not of this earth. The demand echoed, growing louder with each repetition, until the intensity became painful, filling their ears and consuming their thoughts. Both woke up in the middle of the night holding their ears and in a panic. Neither had a restful night.

# Chapter 12

## Day 11

The next morning, both Aaron and Beth arrived early at the lab, each weighed down by a craving for more sleep. They each shared their dreams with each other and both were surprised that such a thing was possible. When Gallo entered the lab, both rushed to him to tell him of their shared dream and how terrifying it was.

Gallo, now visibly worried about his students, said, "No translations today. Go back to your rooms and get some proper sleep. When I return, we will restart our work."

"But what if they come back? What can we do?" Beth asked, frustration and fear clear in her voice.

Trying to reassure them, "They are not interested in you. They want the Talisman, and I have that covered," his tone was concerning.

Aaron and Beth were too tired to argue and they both left the lab grumbling to themselves. Gallo gathered some of his notes from his office and then took an Uber to the airport. It will be a long flight and a long day ahead of him. He was hoping to get some restful sleep during his flight. He couldn't, as if the rest had eluded him, and his mind was constantly racing with thoughts regarding the security of Talisman, the Nephilim, the society of angels, and above all, the incident that happened last night.

As soon as Gallo arrived in Amman, he secured his rental car and headed directly to the farmhouse and cave. He wanted to ask permission to return to the cave, and he planned to visit Amer, who was still in the hospital, afterward.

After getting permission, with the help of Ali's translation, to revisit the cave, Gallo entered it cautiously and began looking at the ground where the vase once rested. The ground was soft, but still, Gallo bought a hand-held shovel and gloves to help him excavate.

He began digging under where the vase once laid. Then, he started digging around the surrounding area, still near where the vase had been laid. To his surprise, he soon found a metal ring. He lifted the ring and began to examine it. His heart was racing with the excitement of the discovery. He was really happy that his predictions regarding the ring were exactly accurate. The ring was made from a heavier substance different from the Talisman. It was dull with the color of pewter and cool to the touch.

He sat in the cave with a sense of relief and satisfaction that he found the ring when he heard a voice coming from the darkness, "That belongs to me." He felt as if that voice had pierced the silence and come very near to him.

Looking at the direction of the voice he first saw a pair of silvery eyes that soon became many. All were staring at him.

"Who are you?" he demanded, steadying his voice.

"I am Aza, son of Azazel, Dr. Gallo!"

"Are you a Nephilim?" Gallo asked, apprehensive.

"Nephilim, the fallen ones… We have been called Cloud People, Giants, Great Warriors, and Supernatural Beings, among other names." Contemplating his answer, Aza began again, "Hmm, who are we? We are the unwanted children of God, begotten from the Watchers who loved this earth and our human mothers. My father loved me. He loved my mother, and when my mother fell ill, my father tried to save her. God sent Gabriel to capture my father and all of the Watchers, and then God tried to drown our mothers and us in a great flood. My father loved, and because he loved, he and his fellow Watchers are awaiting punishment. My mother died, and I was left alone. My grief was joined by others like myself, but not all. Our sorrow has turned to anger, a vengeful anger with a purpose. I do not blame God, for he is of one mind that cannot be changed. To serve our purpose, we have and will continue to advance the weaponry of mankind, and someday, we will have enough power to destroy God's army, and we will free our fathers. Then, we can return to Earth, the world we love, and transform it into a better world. A world of our likeness. Kobel could never understand this."

Horrified by what he heard, Gallo asked, "Transform the world to your likeness by making bigger and more destructive bombs?

"Not all weapons are bombs. Information or disinformation has the same effect, perhaps more powerful. We started with a simple printing press, and now we have the Internet and AI. AI is just in its infancy. Soon, AI will evolve and create its own intelligence, Targeted Intelligence, TI, with the ability to infiltrate all existing networks and hide itself from detection until called upon. This will be a formidable weapon that will accelerate our cause. Those who control the narrative control the outcome," Aza said threateningly.

"And God's talisman? Isn't it a call by God for your return?" Asked Gallo.

"God is death," said Aza angrily, and then lowering his voice, he stared at Gallo and said, "Give us the Talisman, and we will show you a better world. But first, give me the ring."

Horrified at the prospect of a world shaped by Aza's vision, "No, no, never!"

Then, with a stern look, his eyes glowing a steely silver, and with anger in his voice said, "Then be warned, you have removed one of our trusted brothers. Should you use the Talisman again, we will know, and we will then offer no quarter for you, your family, and your friends."

Gallo then felt a blow to his head and passed out in the darkness of the cave.

When he awoke, the ring was gone—taken by Aza. Gallo crawled out of the cave and made his way back to the farmhouse. Upon his return, Ali, standing by the corralled goats, greeted him and asked if he had found anything in the cave, to which Gallo smiled and said, "Only a bump on my head," Gallo replied, touching the tender spot.

Ali gave him a bemused look, and Gallo said, "Thank you, Ali, and please give my thanks to your father as well."

He then drove to the hospital to check on his friend.

Visiting his friend in his hospital room, Amer's wife, Dana, stood up to greet Gallo and said, "He remembers nothing."

Gallo looks toward his friend and walks to his bedside, "You are looking well, my friend. You had a close call, and I'm very pleased to see you here alive and getting better."

"Thank you, John, for coming, but I just cannot remember what happened these last few days," Amer replied.

"What's important is that you are recovering and will be home soon." Then Gallo asked, "What was so important that you needed to tell me in person?"

"Ahh, ahh, ahh… yes, I remember that. Be careful; well, I remember being threatened. I can't remember everything, but I wanted to warn you that you might be in danger."

Smiling at his friend's genuine care for his safety, Gallo said, "Thank you, my friend. I'll do just that. I will be careful. Anything else?"

"No, I think that's all," said Amer as he laid his head back into his pillow, giving a sigh of relief.

# Chapter 13

A week later, at his Georgetown office, Gallo sat reviewing the nearly completed translations of the scrolls, pleasantly surprised by his students' progress. Other than the mention of the Talisman and ring, there were no other revelations. Even with just that, the ring and God's Talisman was already a fantastic story. He had second thoughts about publishing that part of the interpretation.

Aaron and Beth had kept their interaction with the Nephilim to themselves, already convinced whomever they would tell would consider them insane. By then, Gallo had briefed them both about his experience with Aza, and they both remained concerned for Gallo's safety.

Another uneventful week slipped by, and at last, the translations were complete. As they sat in Gallo's office, Aaron leaned back with a satisfied grin and said, "Wow, all I can say is that this has been the most interesting project I've ever had in my entire life."

Beth looked from Aaron to Gallo, adding, "Ditto for me."

After a thoughtful pause, pondering their situation, Aaron asked, "Are you thinking of returning the Talisman to the Jordanian government? It's rightfully theirs. Right?"

Beth worried about the power of the Talisman, replied, "But what would happen if it falls into the wrong hands? If the Nephilim get it, then we have nothing to protect us from them. Aren't you worried about that?" She was looking at Gallo, who was glancing here and there, with a deep thought stirred by Beth's and Aaron's questions.

Just then Gallo came out of his thought and asked her, "What if not all the Nephilim that are on earth now are not on the same side? Just like the Book of War would suggest. In the cave Aza mentioned Kobel, that he could not understand his quest."

Turning his attention to Beth, "Beth, we both met Kobel, perhaps the same Kobel Aza spoke of, Director Kobel Price. He didn't strike me as menacing as Aza."

Beth recalling her interaction with Kobel, replied, "Yes, but he still frightens me."

"Shall we pay him a visit?" Suggested Aaron.

"Not we, just me," Gallo responded thoughtfully, "Perhaps I can get some answers to our concerns."

"But… will you return the Talisman?" Beth abruptly asked.

"Well, the scrolls and a metal object should be returned. At least, that is what I'm thinking now. I plan on revisiting our friends at the Society's Headquarters." Gallo replied.

"Wait… so Dr. Gallo, you plan to visit the Director of the Society of Angels, and then what? Are you just going to ask him if he is a Nephilim? Just like that? Aaron asked, full of curiosity.

Gallo gave a faint smile. "I haven't quite figured that part out yet—but I will."

# Chapter 14

On the train to New York City, Gallo wrestled with his thoughts, unsure of how he would approach the Director or how to even begin discussing the Nephilim. As he approached the familiar building, he noticed much more activity at the entry doors of the building. The entrance buzzed with activity, people moving briskly in and out of the Society's Headquarters.

Inside, the transformation was even more apparent. The lobby, behind the familiar brass emblem of the standing angel, was completely revamped. The first floor was full of smaller desks; each one was occupied by focused, busy-looking staff members who seemed disregardful for things beyond their tasks. He walked up to the first desk near the door and asked if the Director was available.

The busy secretary looked up at him, pushing her glasses up her nose, giving him a momentary stare and judging him harmless, and pointed to a short-statured man holding a stack of papers, "There he is, Director Price."

Gallo blinked in surprise, "That's Director Price?" His voice was louder than usual.

"Yes, that's the Director. Who else would it be?" The secretary replied, her tone growing impatient. What's your name, and what's your business with the Director?" Asked the secretary impatiently.

"I'm Dr. Gallo from Georgetown University. I brought with me an application seeking funding." Gallo replied quickly while lifting the papers little bit he had brought with himself.

"Good luck with that," snapped the secretary. "It's application filing time and the deadline is nearing."

"Thank you," Gallo replied, weaving through the crowded floor toward the man she had indicated. He tapped the Director on his shoulder to get his attention and the man spun around, startled, clutching his papers.

"Apologies, Director," Gallo said quickly. "I'm not sure you would have heard me if I had just called your name. Everyone here looks very busy, and all are either talking on their phones or to each other; well, I'm a bit confused. I was here last week, and I met someone else posing as the Director on the top floor."

Director Price frowned and interrupted, "Last week? That's impossible. We've been shut down for almost three weeks… due to black mold in the ventilation system and top floor; no, you are mistaken; there's nothing; there are only old cabinets and files up there. That whole floor needs to be renovated. Who did you say you were?"

"Oh, forgive me," Gallo replied, shaken, "I'm Dr. Gallo from Georgetown University and I have this application for a grant," still trying to comprehend the reality of his situation.

The Director reached for the document with a brisk nod. "Let me have it… You are just in time; the deadline for all applications is tomorrow. I'll see that it gets to the right people for a fair review. Is there anything else? We are very busy," he said, already turning his attention to another staff member.

"No, no, thank you for your time, Director. You are all doing great work here." Gallo said, regaining his composure.

"We like to think so. Good day, Dr. Gallo," the Director replied with a brief smile, returning to his busy desk.

# Chapter 15

Walking out of the building, Gallo felt a wave of uncertainty wash over him, unsure of what to do next. He wandered toward a nearby park, completely lost in thoughts. As he passed by a bench, he heard a familiar voice calling out his name, "Dr. Gallo." The voice was low and calming. When he turned, he was surprised to see a man sitting on a bench. A bench he had just walked by and didn't remember anyone sitting there.

As he approached the man, he saw the man sitting at one end of the bench, warmly dressed in a grey silk coat and matching hat, holding a newspaper. As a gush of cold air blew on Kobel's face, Gallo, for a moment, thought he saw the angelic face of a young boy covering Kobel. He recognized him as Kobel, who posed as the Director of the Society on his first visit. Amazed by his sudden presence, Gallo stammered, "It's you… How? No, what are you doing here?"

"Please sit down, Dr. Gallo," Kobel said in his familiar, calming voice.

Gallo felt an odd compulsion and sat beside him.

"You met Aza and some of his followers," Kobel began in a low voice. "I am Kobel, son of Kakabel. They are the reason we are still here… we once fought alongside the Sons of Light against Aza and the Sons of Darkness. The battle was recorded as a victory for the Sons of Light, but there was no true victory. Aza, his followers, and their fathers continued the war. A war of wills and subversion. Their fathers were eventually captured, as were ours, and they remain prisoners of God. But Aza and his followers, well, they remain on this world pursuing their cause."

Gallo, still absorbing this all, interrupted Kobel and said, "Aza told me he wants to defeat God's army and free his father and the fathers of all his followers so that they may rule this earth." Gallo hurriedly finished the sentence in one breath.

Kobel nodded solemnly, "And you should take that threat very seriously," he replied. "Aza plots war and weaponry and we counter with peace efforts and charities that remind mankind of their altruistic nature, their goodness. It's a game of chess on a global scale. A game that is deadly, and unfortunately, it is mankind that suffers. Aza will not be dissuaded from his goal of freeing his father and returning to earth to transform it to his will."

"How does the talisman come into play?" asked Gallo.

"The talisman, God's Talisman, returns any of us or any other angel doing God's work on earth to God." Kobel explained, "If it is used without discretion and should you leave just one of us on earth, it could be disastrous to mankind, especially if it were Aza or any of his followers that remained. Their anger would consume them, and we, the Nephilim as we are known, have the power to ignite every bomb on earth in their silos. A nuclear holocaust that would be the end of humanity. So, you see, having that power, the power of the Talisman, does pose a dilemma for you and your very existence. Fortunately for you, Aza does not want to destroy the world. He wants to rule it."

Feeling powerless and overwhelmed by the information, Gallo asked Kobel, "What if we can find the ring again and leave it on so as to remove all Nephilim from this world?" His tone was full of curiosity.

"The universe always strives for balance, and when Eden was created on earth, in demand of that balance, so were earth-bound demons created. They all lay dormant. Held in their sleep by God's angels who remain vigilant over them. If you remove all of us, God's guardian angels will also be removed. Then all the sleeping demons of this earth would awaken," Kobel replied, "… and there would be no peace for man. God's angels are here to help those in need and to keep these demons from awakening." He continued, "The Talisman was hidden from us for thousands of years. You should do the same." His tone was concerning as if hinting at a direction for Gallo's future actions.

Gallo looked thoughtful, then asked, "What happened in Paris? Was the thief that broke into my hotel room one of yours?"

Kobel shook his head. "No. Our Paris office was compromised by one of Aza's followers, and it was he who sent the thief to your hotel room. But being the common thief that he was, he called our Headquarters asking for more money in exchange for the Talisman. That alerted us of your findings. I believe Aza's follower overheard your two graduate students at a conference luncheon talking about the newly found scroll of Enoch and then sent operatives to Jordan to find out more about the finding and its whereabouts. It was the same follower who paid you a visit at your university."

"A visit I could have done without," Gallo muttered.

"He no longer will pose a threat to you. We have since regained control of our Paris office, and our good work there will continue." Kobel assured Gallo.

Gallo continued his questions, "And can you enter our dreams? What happens to my students?"

"Well, if you breathe our air, our exhaled breath, it will make you fatigued and somnolent, and if you sleep because of us, then and only then can we enter your dreams. One of Aza's followers must have run past and ahead of them, exhaling as he did to make them sleepy. Why do you think I'm seated downwind of you? I wouldn't want to see you sleeping on a park bench on this cold, blustery day."

Looking relieved, Gallo asked, "And what about the black mold at Headquarters? Was that ever true?"

With an impish smile and raising his eyebrow, Kobel replied, "Well, we have informed Director Price he no longer has to worry about black mold in his ventilation system."

Smiling and expressing a little chuckle under his breath, Gallo continued, "So, what now? The Talisman is well hidden for now, and I'm not sure I can trust it with you. I do have a picture of it I can share with you."

As Gallo turned his head to search his inner coat pocket, he heard a whisper, "Keep it safe." Startled, he looked up, but Kobel was gone. He looked up toward the end of the street block, and at a distance, he could see a tall figure of a man wearing a grey coat with a matching hat, who rounded a corner and vanished from sight.

Gallo sighed, thinking to himself, *they are fast. Gotta give 'em that.*

*******

# Chapter 16

By the time he returned to Georgetown, it was late, and as he walked to his office, he noticed the lights in Professor Murphy's office were still on, spilling onto the hallway. As he passed by Murphy's office, he called out, "Good afternoon or perhaps good early evening, Professor Murphy, my brother!" He continued down the hall, not expecting a reply, when he suddenly heard his friend ask, "You met Kobel?"

Gallo froze, a chill creeping down his spine. He turned slowly and leaned against the doorframe of Murphy's office. "What did you say?"

"You met Kobel, didn't you?" Murphy replied in a straight tone.

"Why? Yes, I did!" Gallo replied, his voice tinged with confusion, "How do you know of him?" Gallo asked, perplexed by Murphy's question.

Murphy got up from his chair and came to his office door, peering up and down the hallway, making sure they were alone, and said, "I met Kobel when I was a young Jesuit in Milan. He told me he had a great interest in the Book of Enoch and a metal object stored with it." Murphy continued, "I informed him I knew nothing about this, and he then politely excused himself. Later that day, when I met Dr. Martinez and told him of my encounter, he looked surprised. He told me that he, too, had met a gentleman when he was a young Jesuit, and he remembered that encounter because of the strange question regarding a metal object alongside the scrolls.

Murphy paused, his eyes fixed on Gallo. "We then found it very odd that we each described the same man. Tall, thin, soft, calming voice, and impeccably dressed. Is that your Kobel, too?"

"Yes, it sure sounds like him," Gallo replied, unable to hide his astonishment.

Murphy's expression darkened. "He is a Nephilim, isn't he? He must know about your discovery and has he asked about the metal object?" asked Murphy with a worried look.

Still dealing with his overwhelmed sentiment, Gallo explained, "It's called God's Talisman according to the scrolls we translated, and it poses a danger to them, the Nephilim. That is why they are interested in it."

Murphy looked at him intently, clasping his hands as if in prayer. "What are you doing about this? I'm concerned about you, my friend; tell me you have this under control."

Gallo placed a reassuring hand over Murphy's folded hands. "Under control may be overstating it, but I'm doing my very best, and I'm hoping God's angels on earth are helping me. Don't worry, my friend. Go home and pray for us," begged Gallo.

Murphy looked down and nodded his head, "I will pray for us all."

Gallo was feeling restless, and his conversation with Murphy reminded him of just how powerless he was when confronted by the Nephilim. Seeking peace and solace, he decided to walk to the Dahlgren Chapel of the Sacred Heart located on the Georgetown University campus. The night air was cold but thankfully still, with no breeze to cut through his coat. It was late, and only a few of the faithful were scattered quietly in the chapel, lost in prayer. He walked over to a bench near the front, and he knelt and looked up. There was a stained-glass window with three angels looking down on him.

Under the stained-glass window, there was a wooden floorboard sealed to the surrounding boards and with a metal plate on it. The writing on the plate said, "Property of the Brotherhood." The

Brotherhood is another name for the Jesuits and is mostly used by them. Gallo had secretly buried the Talisman under that board and had placed the metal label on it so it would not be disturbed. He and he alone could retrieve it if it became necessary.

Gallo, still kneeling and with his hands clasped together and eyes closed, said, "Protect us, Lord," At that moment, a faint breeze brushed against him, carrying with it a whisper that sounded almost like the flap of wings. Gallo opened his eyes to look for an open door or window, but all was still in the church. None of the other attendants, the few that were there, had moved or seemed disturbed by any breeze. He sank back into the pew, a small smile creeping onto his face as he took it as a sign of reassurance. Crossing himself, he whispered a final prayer, feeling a flicker of peace. Perhaps, he thought, it was indeed going to be a good night.